ARTY
the SMARTY

WHY THIS IS AN EASY READER

- This story has been carefully written to keep the young reader's interest high.

- It is told in a simple, open style, with a strong rhythm that adds enjoyment both to reading aloud and silent reading.

- There is a very high percentage of words repeated. It is this skillful repetition which helps the child to read independently. Seeing the words again and again, he "practices" the vocabulary he knows, and learns with ease the words that are new.

- Only 164 different words have been used, with plurals and root words counted once.

  Almost half of the words in this story have been used at least three times.

  About one-quarter of the words have been used at least seven times.

  Some words have been used between 20 and 40 times.

ABOUT THIS STORY

- This story has fresh humor, a great deal of action, and tells an unusual tale. Young readers will find themselves very much involved with the doings of Arty.

ARTY
the SMARTY

Story by FAITH McNULTY
Pictures by ALBERT AQUINO
Editorial Consultant: LILIAN MOORE

GROSSET & DUNLAP
Publishers
New York, N. Y. 10010

Introduction

These books are meant to help the young reader discover what a delightful experience reading can be. The stories are such fun that they urge the child to try his new reading skills. They are so easy to read that they will encourage and strengthen him as a reader.

The adult will notice that the sentences aren't too long, the words aren't too hard, and the skillful repetition is like a helping hand. What the child will feel is: "This is a good story—and I can read it myself!"

For some children, the best way to meet these stories may be to hear them read aloud at first. Others, who are better prepared to read on their own, may need a little help in the beginning—help that is best given freely. Youngsters who have more experience in reading alone—whether in first or second or third grade—will have the immediate joy of reading "all by myself."

These books have been planned to help all young readers grow—in their pleasure in books and in their power to read them.

Lilian Moore
Specialist in Reading
Formerly of Division of Instructional Research,
New York City Board of Education

This is the story
of a little fish.
His name was Arty
and he was a smarty.

One day all the little fish
were swimming side by side.

Little fish like to swim

the same way at the same time.

So the little fish all swam this way.

Then they all swam that way.

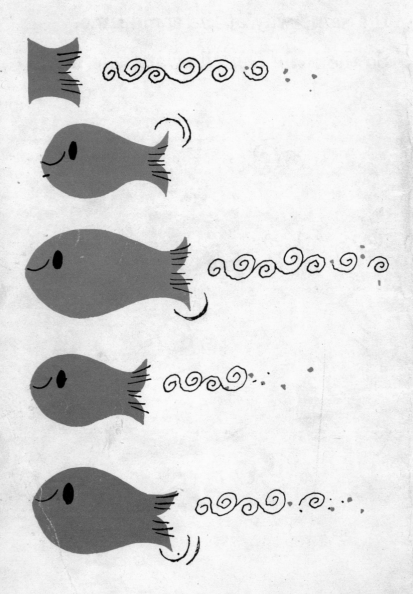

What did Arty the Smarty do?
When the fish went this way,
Arty went that way.

When the fish went that way,
Arty went this way.

12

Soon the little fish
were all mixed up.

Then the fish began to swim
together again.
This way.

That way.

Along came Arty the Smarty again.

What did he do?

This time he was upside down.

He was making a funny fish face.

All the little fish began to laugh.

Bloooooo — Bloooooooo — Blooooo —

They all made laugh bubbles.

And they got all mixed up again!

One day Arty saw some
little fish crying.

Mean Old Crab made them cry.

The little fish were afraid

of Mean Old Crab.

Not Arty!

Arty swam up to the old crab.
Mean Old Crab was eating
his dinner.

Arty took hold of Crab's dinner.

Then he pulled.

Old Crab wanted his dinner.

So he did not let go.

Arty pulled and pulled.
He pulled the crab around
and around.

Mean Old Crab was dizzy.

He had to let go.

He was so dizzy he went around
and around, till he was far away.

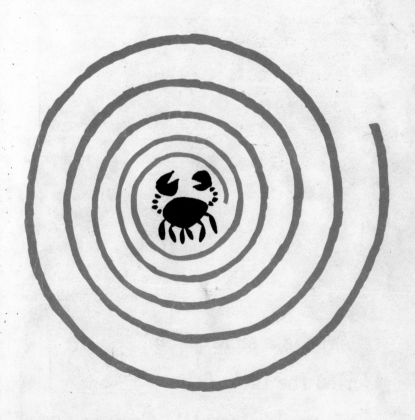

"Arty is a smarty!"

cried the little fish.

"He made Mean Old Crab go away!"

One day Arty saw something
on a hook.
The hook was on a line.

And away up there a fisherman
was holding that line.

Yummy! There was something
good to eat on that hook.
Arty swam over.

"No! No!" cried the little fish.

"Arty, do not go near that hook!"

But Arty was a smarty.

He knew a way to get the food

right off the hook.

And he did.

Then he put something on the hook
for the fisherman.

Soon the hook came down again.

Yummy! More good food!

Arty swam over to get it.

"No, Arty! NO!"

cried the little fish.

"Do not go near the hook!"

But Arty knew what to do!
He took the food off again.

Again he put something on the hook
for the fisherman.

38

Up went the hook with the surprise.
All the fish laughed.

But not the fisherman!

He went away.

"Arty is some smarty,"

the little fish cried.

"He made the fisherman go away!

Arty can do anything!"

But there was something Arty
could not do.
More than anything,
Arty wanted to make a BIG splash.

But he was a little fish.

All he could make was

a little splash.

Arty did not stop trying.

He jumped and jumped.

He just HAD to make a big splash.

A big BIG splash!

He jumped and jumped.
But all he could make was
a little splash.

One day Arty said,

"I need more room to make

a big splash.

I will swim out to sea."

"No, no, Arty,"
cried the little fish.
"Do not go out to sea.
You will not come back!"

47

But Arty swam out to sea.

Way out at sea

there were fishing boats.

Way out at sea

there were nets to catch fish.

"Not me!" said Arty the Smarty.

He was a little fish.

He swam in and out of the nets.

And on he went,

out to the deepest deep of the sea.

Arty did not know it, but whales
live in the deepest deep of the sea.
And a big big whale was
swimming by.
He was so big.
His mouth was like a barn door.
And his mouth was open so wide
that Arty did not see the whale.

On came the whale.

On went Arty,

right into the whale's big mouth.

It was deep and dark

inside the whale.

Arty did not like it.

"Where am I?" he said.

"What is this? What's going on?"

Arty began swimming
around and around,
here and there,
this way and that.

Bump! Bump!

He hit the sides of the whale.

Arty began to jump and splash.

Blooo—Blooo—Blooo—

He began to blow bubbles, too.

Bump! Bump!

Splash! Splash!

Bloooooo! Bloooo!

The whale did not know

what was going on inside.

All he could feel

was tickle, tickle, tickle, tickle.

All at once the whale had to laugh.
What a laugh that was!

Out came Arty

in a big, BIG, BIG splash!

"I did it! I did it!"

cried Arty.

"I made a whale of a splash!"

And he swam home
as fast as he could
to tell the little fish all about it.

CHOOSE FROM THESE EASY READERS

5901 Will You Come to My Party?

5902 Hurry Up, Slowpoke

5903 Mr. Pine's Mixed-Up Signs

5904 The Adventures of Silly Billy

5905 The Secret Cat

5906 Billy Brown Makes Something Grand

5907 Miss Polly's Animal School

5908 The Duck on the Truck

5909 A Train for Tommy

5910 Surprise in the Tree

5911 The Monkey in the Rocket

5912 Billy Brown: The Baby Sitter

5913 Fly-Away at the Air Show

5914 Arty the Smarty

5915 The Surprising Pets of Billy Brown

5916 Barney Beagle

5917 I Made a Line

5918 Laurie and the Yellow Curtains

5919 Grandpa's Wonderful Glass

5920 Benjamin in the Woods

5921 Barney Beagle Plays Baseball

5922 The Day Joe Went to the Supermarket

5923 Question and Answer Book

5924 Jokes and Riddles

5925 Let Papa Sleep!

5926 The Surprise in the Story Book

5927 The Big Green Thing

5928 The Boy Who Fooled the Giant

5929 More Jokes and Riddles

5930 Too Many Pockets

5931 The Clumsy Cowboy

5932 Cat in the Box

5933 How the Animals Get to the Zoo

5934 The Birthday Party

5935 Little Gray Mouse and the Train

5936 Mr. Pine's Purple House

5937 When I Grow Up

5938 One Kitten is not Too Many

5939 How to Find a Friend

5940 The Boy, the Cat and the Magic Fiddle

5941 Little Gray Mouse Goes Sailing

5942 Keep Your Eyes Open

5945 Old Man and the Tiger

5946 Barbie Goes to a Party

5947 Barney Beagle and the Cat

5948 What's Going on Here?

5949 Little Popcorn

5951 The Fox Who Traveled

5952 The Three Coats of Benny Bunny